MR. QUIET

by Roger Hargreaves

Mr Quiet liked the quiet life.

He lived, quietly, in a small little cottage in the middle of a wood.

The problem was, that small little cottage was in the middle of a wood in the middle of a country called Loudland!

Everything and everybody in Loudland was noisy.

Oh, the noise!

Dogs didn't go "woof" like dogs you know.

They went (take a deep breath) "WOOF!"

People didn't shut their doors like you or I would shut our doors.

They slammed them.

BANG!

People didn't talk to each other.

They shouted at each other.

"HELLO," they'd shout as they met in the street.

And, you've heard about something being as quiet as a mouse, haven't you?

Not in Loudland.

They had the noisiest mice in the world.

"SQUEAK! SQUEAK!" they'd roar at each other.

Mr Noisy would have liked living in Loudland.

He'd have loved it.

But Mr Quiet didn't.

Noise frightened him.

So, he stayed in his cottage in the middle of his wood as much as he could.

But of course he couldn't stay there all the time.

Every week, for instance, he had to go shopping.

He used to creep into the grocer's shop.

"GOOD MORNING," bellowed the grocer.
"WHAT CAN I DO FOR YOU?"

"Please," whispered Mr Quiet, "could I have some cornflakes please?"

"WHAT?"

"Cornflakes. Please," he whispered.

"SPEAK UP!"

Mr Quiet tried his loudest whisper.

"Cornflakes."

"CAN'T HEAR YOU," shouted the grocer. "NEXT PLEASE!"

And poor Mr Quiet had to creep away without any cornflakes.

It wasn't fair, was it?

He crept into the butcher's.

"Please," he whispered, "I'd like some meat."

The butcher didn't even hear him.

He was humming to himself, loudly and fiercely.

Mr Quiet tried again.

"Please," he whispered, "I'd like some meat."

The butcher started to whistle.

It sounded more like a burglar alarm than a whistle.

Mr Quiet fled.

Empty handed.

It often happened, which probably explains why he was so little.

Poor Mr Quiet.

He sat at home that night with a feeling of despair.

"Whatever am I to do?" he thought.

"It's no use," he thought, "I'll just have to try again."

And so, the following day, he went shopping again.

But, the same thing happened.

"CAN'T HEAR YOU," thundered the grocer. "NEXT PLEASE!"

"CAN'T HEAR YOU," bellowed the greengrocer. "NEXT PLEASE!"

"CAN'T HEAR YOU," roared the milkman. "NEXT PLEASE!"

"CAN'T HEAR YOU," boomed the butcher. "NEXT PLEASE!"

Oh dear!

Poor Mr Quiet went home and went to bed.

Hungry.

The morning after he was awakened by a noise which sounded like bombs dropping.

It was the Loudland postman knocking at Mr Quiet's door.

BANG! BANG! BANG! BANG!

Mr Quiet went and opened the door.

"MORNING," shouted the postman. "LETTER FOR YOU!"

Mr Quiet took the letter into his kitchen.

He sat down to open it.

He waited until the noise of the postman's footsteps died away.

CLUMP CLUMP CLUMP CLUMP clump clump.

Mr Quiet opened the letter in great excitement.

He'd never had a letter before.

It was from Mr Happy in Happyland.

An invitation!

To stay!

Mr Quiet was overjoyed.

He rushed upstairs and packed his bag and set off that very morning.

It was late when he arrived on Mr Happy's doorstep.

He knocked on Mr Happy's door.

Tap tap tap.

Mr Happy opened the door.

"Hello," he smiled. "I thought I heard something. You must be Mr Quiet. Well, don't just stand there, come in and have some supper."

It was the first proper meal Mr Quiet had had for months. And while he was eating it he told Mr Happy all about the problems he'd been having in Loudland.

Mr Happy was most sympathetic.

Over breakfast the following morning, Mr Happy told Mr Quiet that he'd been thinking about his problem.

"I think," he said, "that under the circumstances you'd better stay here in Happyland."

Mr Quiet's face lit up.

"And," continued Mr Happy, "we'll find you a house, and," he went on, "a job."

Mr Quiet's face dropped.

"I'm not very good at jobs," he confessed, "because I'm too quiet."

"Ah," smiled Mr Happy. "I have the very job for a quiet chap like you!"

And so, the very next day, Mr Quiet started work.

And he loves it.

Do you know where he works?

In the Happy Lending Library!

As you know, everybody who goes into a library has to be very quiet, and only whispering is allowed.

What a clever idea of Mr Happy's, wasn't it?

And these days, Mr Quiet is as happy as can be.

Why, only the other day, do you know what he did on his way home from work?

He was so happy he laughed out loud.

Can you imagine?

Tee hee hee!

"NEXT PLEASE!"

Fantastic offers for Mr. Men fans!

Collect all your Mr. Men or Little Miss books in these superb durable collectors' cases!

Only £5.99 inc. postage and packing, these wipe-clean, hard-wearing cases will give all your Mr. Men or Little Miss books a beautiful new home!

Keep track of your collection with this giant-sized double-sided Mr. Men and Little Miss Collectors' poster.

Collect 6 tokens and we will send you a brilliant giant-sized double-sided collectors' poster! Simply tape a £1 coin to cover postage and packaging in the space provided and fill out the form overleaf.

STICK £1 COIN HERE (for poster only)

Only need a few Mr. Men or Little Miss to complete your set? You can order any of the titles on the back of the books from our Mr. Men order line on 0870 787 1724. Orders should be delivered between 5 and 7 working days.

--- **TO BE COMPLETED BY AN ADULT** ---

To apply for any of these great offers, ask an adult to complete the details below and send this whole page with the appropriate payment and tokens, to: MR. MEN CLASSIC OFFER, PO BOX 715, HORSHAM RH12 5WG

☐ Please send me a giant-sized double-sided collectors' poster.

AND ☐ I enclose 6 tokens and have taped a £1 coin to the other side of this page.

☐ Please send me ☐ Mr. Men Library case(s) and/or ☐ Little Miss library case(s) at £5.99 each inc P&P

☐ I enclose a cheque/postal order payable to Egmont UK Limited for £...............

OR ☐ Please debit my MasterCard / Visa / Maestro / Delta account (delete as appropriate) for £...............

Card no. ☐☐☐☐☐☐☐☐☐☐☐☐☐☐☐☐☐☐ Security code ☐☐☐

Issue no. (if available) ☐ Start Date ☐☐/☐☐/☐☐ Expiry Date ☐☐/☐☐/☐☐

Fan's name: .... Date of birth: ....

Address: ....
....
.... Postcode: ....

Name of parent / guardian: ....

Email for parent / guardian: ....

Signature of parent / guardian: ....

Please allow 28 days for delivery. Offer is only available while stocks last. We reserve the right to change the terms of this offer at any time and we offer a 14 day money back guarantee. This does not affect your statutory rights. Offers apply to UK only.

☐ We may occasionally wish to send you information about other Egmont children's books. If you would rather we didn't, please tick this box.

Ref: MRM 001

cut along the dotted line and return this whole page